DARK STAR

MIDNIGHT
DARK STAR

R.T. MARTIN

darbycreek
MINNEAPOLIS

Darby Creek
A division of Lerner Publishing Group, Inc.
241 First Avenue North
Minneapolis, MN 55401 USA

For reading levels and more information, look up this title at www.lernerbooks.com.

The images in this book are used with the permission of: © Illia Balla/123RF.com (meteors); © iStockphoto.com/da-kuk (cliff); © SKY2015/Shutterstock.com (night sky); backgrounds: © iStockphoto.com/AF-studio; © iStockphoto.com/blackred; © iStockphoto.com/Adam Smigielski.

Main body text set in Janson Text LT Std 12/17.5.
Typeface provided by Adobe Systems.

Library of Congress Cataloging-in-Publication Data

Names: Martin, R. T., 1988- author.
Title: Dark star / R.T. Martin.
Description: Minneapolis : Darby Creek, [2017] | Series: Midnight | Summary: "An innocent extra-credit assignment to watch a meteor shower turns dangerous when a student goes missing. Will everyone make it out alive?"— Provided by publisher. | Audience: Age 11-18. | Audience: Grade 9 to 12.
Identifiers: LCCN 2016022759 (print) | LCCN 2016037651 (ebook) | ISBN 9781512427691 (lb : alk. paper) | ISBN 9781512430998 (pb : alk. paper) | ISBN 9781512427899 (eb pdf)
Subjects: | CYAC: Supernatural—Fiction. | Missing persons—Fiction.
Classification: LCC PZ7.1.M37346 Dar 2017 (print) | LCC PZ7.1.M37346 (ebook) | DDC [Fic]—dc23

LC record available at https://lccn.loc.gov/2016022759

Manufactured in the United States of America
1-41494-23355-8/5/2016

CHAPTER 1

THURSDAY 11:00 A.M.

Mr. Petsky dropped the test onto Claire's desk with a big red "F" written at the top. "This is not good, Claire."

She stared at it, feeling sick to her stomach while her teacher wound up and down the rows of desks passing out the rest of the exams. This was bad—really bad. Too many Fs. Claire was definitely failing and she knew it. Her parents were going to demolish her social life when they found out about this.

"At least one of you studied," beamed Mr. Petsky. "Val is the shining star of this class: one hundred percent, plus extra credit. Well done."

Of course Val got an A. She transferred to Middleton High two weeks ago and, ever since then, has only impressed Mr. Petsky. Meanwhile, Claire kept digging her grades into a deeper and deeper ditch. Now she was at the bottom of that pit looking at an impossible climb out.

She had actually tried to study this time. The night before the exam, she read chapters fifteen through eighteen *twice*. How could this have happened? Claire liked Mr. Petsky. He was a good teacher, but he gave really hard tests, and science had never been her strongest subject. She was better at history or English, although she wasn't particularly good at those either.

The bell rang.

"Remember, your next test is in three weeks!" Mr. Petsky shouted over the noise of students getting out of their desks and picking up their books and bags. "I recommend asking Val to study with you. Have a good day."

Claire left the room in silence with her head down and a sinking feeling in her chest. She pictured herself studying even harder for the next test and still getting it back with another "F" at the top. Even if she did manage to pass it, there may be nothing she could do to salvage her overall grade.

"Claire! Claire!" Cooper was running down the hallway toward her. He had done this—run down the hall at full speed—every time he saw her since the fourth grade when they met. "How'd you do on the test?" As usual, he was out of breath.

"Another F. I don't think I can pass the class anymore."

"There's still one more test though, right?"

"Yeah," Claire said. "But I think I've failed too many now. Even if I get an A on it, that wouldn't be enough for me to pass the whole class."

"What are you going to do?" He nearly had his breath back.

"Hope my parents don't kill me."

They reached Claire's locker, and she started spinning the lock.

"Hey, Emma!" Cooper shouted. "Claire's failing science!"

Claire quickly turned around. "Coop! If you want everyone to know, why don't you just use the PA system?"

Emma came over from her locker just down the hall. "Mr. Petsky's nice. He doesn't want anyone to fail. He said that at the beginning of the year. I'm sure he'll give you some project or assignment to do so you can pass." Emma was the logical one between them. Even when they were kids, Emma never thought a problem was as bad as it seemed. She always had a solution.

Books fell out of Claire's bursting locker. Emma stooped down with her to pick them up. "I can help you with it, whatever it is, and we can study together for the last test."

"Thanks," Claire said. "I'm more worried about what my parents are going to do."

"We should do something fun so you can take your mind off it for a bit," Cooper suggested. "Want to see a movie this Saturday?"

"That sounds great," said Claire, turning back to her locker. She could use a little relaxation. School had been nothing but stress recently. It would be nice to do something—anything—fun. It would be great to see a movie, assuming her parents let her, but Claire knew that would be unlikely.

"Are you guys going to the bluffs this weekend?" Claire spun around at the sound of the unfamiliar voice. It was Val. Her sudden appearance made both Emma and Cooper jump.

"Geez, what are you, a ninja?" said Cooper, holding his chest.

Claire closed her locker and zipped up her bag. "Why would we be going to the bluffs?"

"I told Mr. Petsky about a meteor shower that's going to happen at midnight on Saturday, and he liked the idea of organizing a bunch of students to go watch it as an extra credit assignment," Val said. "He gave out permission slips a week ago."

Claire remembered getting the permission slip, but she'd long since lost it, tossed it in a folder and never seen it again. Why waste a perfectly good Saturday night watching lights for school, much less for her least favorite subject? "No, we're not going to that."

Val's eyes narrowed. "Maybe you should. You of all people could use an extra science lesson." That was uncalled for. This was the first time Val and Claire had ever spoken to each other. She had no business insulting Claire's grades. How did she even know Claire was failing anyway? Claire glared at Val, but quickly looked away. There was something about the way Val looked at her that made Claire uneasy. Val's eyes never seemed to move. They were locked on Claire's face.

"I wouldn't mind going," Cooper blurted out. "I love the bluffs."

"You *would* like one of the creepiest places in Middleton," said Emma.

Val turned to lock eyes with Cooper. "You should come." Val was standing too close to him. It was awkward. He took a step back, but Val took a step forward at the same time. Cooper looked like an animal being backed into a corner.

"Uhh, I think I'll pass," said Cooper, nervously trying to look anywhere but at Val. "Besides, I didn't get my permission slip in."

"If your parents call Mr. Petsky, it would be fine," Val said. Cooper's back was up against the lockers now. "If you don't go, you'll regret it."

Sounds like a threat, Claire thought.

"We've got plans anyway," Cooper said. He was starting to sweat.

There was something off about Val. Maybe it was just because she was a new student and the only thing Claire knew about her was that she was amazing at science class, but there was still something concerning about her. For one thing, she was incredibly pale. Her veins were clearly visible beneath the skin on her face. It reminded Claire of the skin on corpses she had seen in crime shows on TV. Val's eyes were too steady and her movements too rigid. She seemed robotic.

"Unacceptable," said Val, scowling.

"Whoa," Emma said, ignoring Val's comment. "You've got a tattoo?" Val's shirt sleeve was rolled halfway up her left arm, revealing the bottom of a tattoo that reached her wrist. A group of squares and lines were inked onto Val's skin. Some of the squares were smaller and some were larger, but they were all neatly arranged.

"My parents would never let me get a tattoo!" Cooper said, sliding sideways along the lockers, trying to escape Val. She took another step toward him.

Val rolled her sleeve down. "Oh, that. That's nothing," she said.

"I like it," said Emma, clearly trying to be polite, although she seemed a little uneasy as well. "Does it mean something?"

Val turned and locked her eyes on Emma. She grinned. "You'll see."

CHAPTER 2

3:00 P.M.

Claire got home after school, tossed her backpack next to the closet by the door, and scratched Milo, her family's golden retriever, behind the ears as he greeted her. "Good boy," she said. "Want to switch lives with me for the next week or so?" Milo tilted his head and walked away. "Well, thanks anyway."

"Claire?" It was her dad calling from the kitchen. "Come in here right now."

She recognized the tone. It was the same tone he used when he told her she couldn't go on the class trip to the amusement park because she had gotten a D on a math test. Did he already know about her science grade, or was he mad about something else? Claire tried to think of what else she had done wrong but couldn't come up with anything, at least not that had happened recently or that he didn't already know about.

In the kitchen, her dad was seated at the counter, and her mom was leaning against the cabinets. Both of them had stern looks.

"I just got off the phone with Mr. Petsky," said her dad. Claire's stomach tied itself into a knot. He had actually called her parents. This was about as bad as it could get. "You failed another test. How many is that?"

"I don't know," she mumbled.

"Four. That's what Mr. Petsky told me." When he was mad, Claire's dad liked to ask questions he already knew the answer to.

"You're failing the class right now," her mom said. "There's only one more test, and you may not be able to pass science even if you get an A on it."

"I'm sorry," Claire said. "I studied really hard this time. I'm just not good at science."

"Science is hard for a lot of kids, but they still manage to pass the class. You, on the other hand, need extra credit to offset your embarrassingly low grade," her dad said. "You're lucky Mr. Petsky is holding a trip this Saturday to the bluffs to watch a meteor shower. You're going on that trip to get the extra credit you need, and if you manage to do decently on the last test, he said you'll squeak by with a passing grade. That way you won't have to repeat the class."

"I was going to see a movie with Cooper and Emma this Saturday."

"Not anymore, you're not." The suggestion that she wanted to go to a movie rather than to the bluffs for extra credit made her dad even angrier, and there was no arguing with him when he was like this. "You're going to the bluffs, and that's final. You need the extra credit, so it's decided."

"But the permission slip—I lost it, and you haven't signed it."

"We personally told Mr. Petsky that you could go," said her dad. "You don't need the permission slip, and I'm not arguing about this anymore." He picked up his phone and started scrolling through something. Claire knew the discussion was over.

But she didn't want to give up. "Please don't make me go there. It's—I don't like the bluffs."

The bluffs were a few miles outside of Middleton. They were high up at the top of a series of steep hills that overlooked the entire town. They were also home to an incredibly thick forest. There were clearings, places you could sit and watch the sky, but a large portion of the bluffs was covered in trees. The bluffs were the last place she wanted to go, especially on a Saturday night with her teacher and a bunch of other students she may or may not know. She wouldn't want to go there under any circumstances. Claire buried her face in her hands.

"What's wrong, honey?" Her mom had a softer touch, even when she was mad. "Is it because of what happened? It's perfectly safe."

Every time someone mentioned the bluffs, Claire remembered the news stories from just before she started kindergarten. The Middleton High senior class went up into the bluffs for a camping trip right before graduation. When they didn't come back right away the whole town laughed it off. At first everyone said it was probably just the senior class playing a prank, but the longer the kids were missing, the more worried everyone became. After five days, people really started freaking out. They put up posters everywhere. The news had a hotline for any information about the missing kids. People searched for months and months, but the kids were never found. The entire graduating class just disappeared. Eventually, the town moved on. Most people forgot about them, but Claire still remembered. Now whenever she thought about the bluffs, she thought about those missing students and couldn't help but believe that something horrible had happened to them up there.

"The bluffs are creepy," Claire said feebly. "Can't I just watch the meteor shower at home and write a report about it?"

"There's too much light pollution in town," said her dad. "It's a lot darker up there, and you'll be able to see the shower better. You're going, Claire, and I don't want to hear any more about this."

"Besides," said her mom, "your teacher and a lot of your classmates will be with you. Nothing's going to go wrong."

CHAPTER 3

FRIDAY 7:30 A.M.

The next day, Claire grabbed books out of her locker for her first class and heard, “Claire! Claire!” Cooper ran down the hallway as Emma walked behind him. “What movie do you want to see on Saturday? I want to see *Alien Wrath*, but Emma said she won’t go to that.”

“Just for once, can you watch a movie that doesn’t involve aliens?” Emma rolled her eyes.

“They’re out there, Emma,” Cooper said. Then he dramatically added, “We need to know what we’re up against.” He burst into laughter. Even he couldn’t take aliens too seriously.

"I can't go," Claire said. "My parents are making me go to the bluffs to watch the meteor shower with Mr. Petsky. I need the extra credit." She closed her locker and started walking to class. Cooper and Emma followed.

"But the bluffs are so creepy," said Emma.

"That's what makes them awesome," Cooper said. "It's so weird and dark up there. I think they're cool."

"They're not cool, Coop," Emma said. "People disappeared up there. They went up and just—*poof*—vanished."

"Could be alien abductions," Cooper said, winking.

"You watch too many alien movies," said Emma. "They're starting to rot your brain. They probably just got lost and never found their way back."

"Can you guys stop?" Claire said. "I'm already freaked out because I have to go there. And this isn't helping."

"Sorry," Cooper said.

"Wait." Emma grabbed Claire's arm and spun her around. "We'll go with you."

"We'll what?" Cooper looked over at Emma in disbelief.

"We'll go with you," Emma repeated.

"Why?" asked Cooper. "We're not failing." Emma gave him a sharp look.

"You guys don't have to do that," Claire said. "You need permission slips anyway."

"We'll get our parents to call Mr. Petsky," said Emma. "If we say we'll get extra credit for it, what are the odds they'll say no?"

"Seriously, you don't have to," said Claire.

"It won't be so bad if the three of us are there together," Emma said. "It's settled, we're going together."

Claire saw Emma elbow Cooper in the ribs. "Ow, what was that—" he started, but then cut off mid-sentence with the look that Emma was giving him. "Uhh, yeah. We'll definitely go with you."

"Thanks, Emma. Having you guys there would make the trip a lot less painful," Claire said. "And less scary," she added. How awful could it be if her two best friends came with her?

"Hey, it might actually be kind of fun," said Cooper. "Up there in the dark by those freaky woods. I saw a meteor shower when I was five, I think, and it was actually pretty cool."

"It'll be great," said Emma.

They reached room 205, where Claire had history class. "There's only a few minutes before the bell, so I should head inside."

Just then, Val walked by the trio. "See you Saturday night," she said, walking away before any of them could respond.

"Oh, good," Cooper stared after her. "She's weird *and* nosey." Cooper watched Val walk down the hall as a look of suspicion came over his face. "Is it weird that Val told Mr. Petsky about the meteor shower? Why does she care if the class all goes up?"

"I'm sure she was just excited about it," said Emma.

"Or she was trying to show off," Claire mumbled under her breath.

Cooper continued, "But who really cares about science that much? And why does she care if *we* go? She was pretty aggressive about it."

"Maybe she was just trying to make friends," said Emma. "She *is* new here."

"I know *I* don't want to be her friend. She creeps me out," Claire said, turning toward her classroom. "See you guys at lunch?"

"You know it," said Cooper.

As Claire sat at her desk waiting for class to start, Cooper's words kept playing over and over in her mind. Why *had* Val suggested to Mr. Petsky that the class go to the bluffs? She was new, so she didn't know about their freaky history. But, like Cooper said, who really cares about science that much? The more she thought about it, the more it freaked Claire out. Why would Val want her to go to the bluffs late at night, and what was it about that girl that made Claire so uncomfortable? Just thinking about Val made Claire squirm in her seat. Claire was so deep in thought that when the bell rang, she actually jumped in her desk. It was probably just the bluffs. That's what was putting her on edge. Even with Cooper and Emma going with her, the idea of heading up there was terrifying. She pushed the thought to the back of her mind and tried to focus on history class. She didn't need to be forced to take an extra credit trip to some freaky museum late at night too.

CHAPTER 4

SATURDAY 10:30 P.M.

"Try to have fun," said Claire's mom. "I promise it won't be as bad as you think."

Claire got out of the car and closed the door behind her. It was bad enough that she had to waste her Saturday night doing work for science class, but to have to go to the creepiest place in Middleton on top of that was not something she would ever look forward to. "Any last chance of getting out of this?" Claire asked through the open window.

Her mom smiled but shook her head. "I'll pick you up when you get back. Love you."

"Love you too, Mom," said Claire. She watched her mom drive away and very briefly thought to herself, *I could just walk away, not get on the bus, and go see a movie with Emma and Cooper*, but she knew her dad would be furious, and there was no way Emma would ditch the trip for a movie. She was way too responsible to do that. Cooper might though.

"Claire! Claire!" Cooper lived close enough to walk to Middleton High. He ran down the sidewalk to her. "I've got a whole bag full of snacks!" As he came to a stop in front of her, he opened his backpack and started rifling through bags of chips, marshmallows, cookies, and candy.

Claire couldn't help but smile. "That's great. I may be freaked out, but at least I'll be well fed." She started walking to the bus while Cooper zipped his bag back up.

"Emma's waiting for us on the bus," he said. "She just texted me."

They joined the long line of students filing onto the bus. Mr. Petsky stood by the door, checking off names on a list as people got on. As Claire walked by, he said, "Glad you could make it." To Cooper: "I was pleasantly surprised to hear you wanted to join us too. Always happy to have some last minute additions. Hop on."

Cooper slid into the seat next to Emma, and Claire sat right behind them. She took an open spot next to a blond girl that she had never talked to. The girl barely looked up from her phone as Claire took her seat.

Almost immediately after sitting down, Cooper popped back up and faced Claire with his arms propped on the back of the seat. "This is going to be so cool! I'm hoping that we get to see a UFO. If there's one place in town that we'd see one, it'd definitely be the bluffs. I'll bet we see one for sure."

"I'll bet we see a meteor shower, get back on this bus, and go home," said Claire. "I just want to get it all over with so I can go home and not fail science."

"Come on," said Cooper. "This is almost better than a movie. This is kind of a real adventure!"

"I don't want an adventure. I'd rather go to a movie."

Cooper rolled his eyes and sat back down.

The last of the students in line got on the bus and Mr. Petsky climbed aboard, stood by the driver's seat, and addressed the group. "I'm glad you're all here tonight. As you know, the shower is supposed to begin at midnight, but we will arrive at the bluffs at about eleven so that we don't miss a moment of it. I want all of you to pay attention during the shower. Make mental notes of how many meteors you see, how far across the sky they fly, how thick or thin their trails are, and most importantly, what it's like to watch this incredible astronomical event. You'll have to write a one-page report on this, due Monday, to receive the extra credit."

The teacher took a quick glance at the list of names before continuing. "Obviously, it's rather late at night. There aren't any buildings or street lights up in the bluffs, which is perfect for viewing an event like a meteor shower, but I want to warn you, it is going to be nearly pitch-black up there. Please keep any source of light turned off. That includes cell phones. We don't want any light pollution getting in the way of our view. Keep in mind that it's very easy to trip and fall or get lost, so I want you all to be very careful and stay close together. No one should go wandering off alone." The girl next to Claire huddled near the window, still hunched over her screen, her phone vibrating as message after message appeared.

"I also think I should mention," Mr. Petsky continued, "that you won't need your phones anyway. The bluffs are a dead zone. The signal from the cell towers in town doesn't extend up there, so those of you with phones won't get any service. If there is an emergency, tell me and I can radio the driver." He held up a walkie-talkie.

Claire glanced at the blond girl, who sighed at the news. Even as Mr. Petsky was speaking, her phone barely stopped buzzing. When Claire looked back at Mr. Petsky, Val was eerily standing behind him. *Where did she come from?* thought Claire. Mr. Petsky jumped a little when he saw her. "Oh, Val, I didn't see you there. Glad you could join us. You can take the seat here next to me." Before Val sat down, she scanned the students and found Claire, Cooper, and Emma. She looked right at them, the edge of her lips curling upward in a wide grin.

Claire heard Cooper whisper to Emma, "What is she doing here? Little Miss Perfect doesn't need extra credit." Claire wondered the same thing. What could possibly motivate her to go on this trip? Val did say the trip was her idea, but this was probably just another way for her to suck up to Mr. Petsky, not that she needed to at this point. She was clearly his favorite student at Middleton. To Claire, the trip seemed like it was going to be a little bit worse with Val coming along—an extra piece of stress she didn't want to deal with.

"All right," Mr. Petsky said. "Here we go!" The bus started up with a roar and began pulling out of the school parking lot.

The girl next to Claire was slouched down in her seat. "Are you okay?" asked Claire.

The girl straightened up a bit and gave Claire a half smile. "Yeah, I'm fine."

Claire smiled at her. "What's your name?"

"Penny," she replied.

"I'm Claire. It's nice to meet you." The girl nodded but didn't say anything. "I don't want to be here, but I need the extra credit. You too?"

"Yeah," Penny said. "I'll fail if I don't go. My parents said I had to come. But none of my friends needed the extra credit, so they ditched me to go play laser tag instead."

"Ugh, I'm sorry." Claire looked up at Emma and Cooper, thankful that she wasn't alone on the trip. "My parents are making me go too. I hate the bluffs. It's so creepy up there."

"What do you mean it's creepy?" Penny asked.

"Well," Claire paused, looking at her shoes. "Haven't you heard about the seniors that disappeared up there a while back?"

"No, I just moved to Middleton a few years ago. What do you mean they disappeared?" Claire saw worry lines form along Penny's forehead.

"I don't know exactly. They all went up to the bluffs but never came back," Claire said, glancing over at Penny.

Penny was ignoring her buzzing phone now. "Like, gone forever?"

Claire nodded. "But, hey. It's going to be all right. I'll stick by you and make sure nothing happens. Hey, guys." Claire tapped the seat in front of her. Cooper and Emma turned around. "This is Penny. It's cool if she hangs out with us tonight, right?"

Emma smiled and nodded. Cooper, very enthusiastically, said, "Absolutely! I'm Cooper, and this is Emma. Are you hungry?" He tossed a bag of pretzels over the seat to Penny. "You can keep those. I've got a whole bag full of stuff, so just let me know if you're still hungry."

Penny smiled as she opened the package and grabbed a handful of pretzels. "Thank you."

"No problem," said Cooper, sitting back down.

"Don't worry," said Claire. "Just stick by us, and we'll all be fine. We may even pass science class."

Claire and Penny talked while the bus drove, ascending the hills into the bluffs. The farther they got, the darker it became. The lights of Middleton faded as they rose up and away from town. The woods got thicker, and the stars became brighter.

Halfway through the drive, Claire looked toward the front of the bus. In the giant rearview mirror right above the driver, she saw Mr. Petsky sifting through papers and, right next to him, Val looking right back at her.

CHAPTER 5

10:50 P.M.

The bluffs were worse than Claire anticipated. It was almost impossible to see anything. With Mr. Petsky's "no light pollution" rule, it was pitch black. When they stepped off the bus, Penny turned to Claire and asked, "Was this the same spot they disappeared from?" Penny looked around. "Those seniors you were talking about?"

"No, I don't think so," Claire lied. She didn't really know, but she didn't want to think that they were in the same spot where a big group of people up and vanished.

Once everyone was off the bus, it turned around and drove back down to the bottom of the bluffs. Penny looked longingly after the disappearing taillights.

"Whoa. Now *this* is dark!" said Cooper.

"How are we going to be able to see without light?" Claire asked.

"Don't worry," said Emma. "Our eyes will adjust in a few minutes." That was Emma, prepared with an answer to everything. They stood around, letting the outlines of the bluffs come into view around them as their eyes got used to the darkness. Once they could see enough to not run into one another, Emma turned to Claire, Cooper, and Penny. "I've got a blanket in my bag that we can all sit on. Should we pick a spot?" They walked over to the clearing and Emma unrolled a large blanket onto the grass, smoothed it out, and invited the others to take a seat.

"Whoa," said Cooper. He had wandered away from them over toward the trees. "Check out these woods!" He and some other students were looking at the forest that lined the bluffs.

The woods were very thick and gnarled—a tangled mess. It was even darker in there than it was in the clearing, and the clearing was too dark for Claire's taste.

"Everyone find a space and get settled," Mr. Petsky shouted to the entire group. "Cooper, stay out of the woods. You won't be able to see the shower in there, so there's no reason to go in. Plus, you could get lost, and knowing you, you *would* get lost." Mr. Petsky smiled to let Cooper know it was only a friendly joke, although there was little chance Cooper would actually be offended. He was fairly immune to criticism.

"You got it," said Cooper. He returned to the girls and started unloading snacks onto the blanket.

They all looked up at the sky. In the deep dark of the bluffs, they could see far more stars than were visible in town, thousands of them spread all across the sky. Soon they'd start flying and streaking across it. Penny seemed nervous, looking through the dark like she expected to see something suddenly appear. Or disappear.

"Are you guys having fun?" Val had snuck up on them again. "I like it up here." She had an odd smile on her face.

"It's fine, I guess," said Claire. No one else said anything.

Val locked eyes with Penny. "You look scared."

"I'm not scared," Penny replied, sitting up a little taller.

Val smirked just like she had when Emma asked about her tattoo. "I think I may have something that will help." She dropped her bag on the ground without breaking eye contact with Penny. When it hit the grass, the bag made a sound like it was filled with glass bottles. She opened it and pulled something out. "Here, take one of these. It's a pin. You should wear it."

In Val's hand was a pin in the shape of a star. It looked like it was made of black glass. In the center of the star was a glowing red light.

Claire took it from Val and turned it over in her hand. It was just an average pin. It felt heavy and cold, but there wasn't anything else truly strange about it. Still, Claire couldn't put her finger on why, but she didn't like it.

Cooper snatched it away from her. "I've seen this before—this exact design! Where did you get this?"

Val didn't answer Cooper's question. She just said, "Go ahead. Wear it."

Cooper handed the pin to Penny who also turned it over a few times in her hand.

"I have enough for everybody," said Val, pulling more of them out of her bag.

"Uhh, no thanks," said Cooper. Emma and Claire both agreed—they didn't want one.

Val frowned and seemed a little annoyed at their refusal. "Fine," she said, as she turned and walked away toward where Mr. Petsky was setting up a lawn chair.

"That girl is so weird," said Cooper.

"It was nice of her to give that pin to Penny, though," said Emma. "Are you going to wear it?"

"Yeah, I think so," said Penny. "It can't hurt to be more visible, right?"

Penny pinned the star to her shirt, the faint red glow from the pin a steady red light. She sat quietly but seemed to be less nervous. She even laughed when Cooper stuck two pieces of licorice in his mouth and clapped his arms like a walrus. Then Penny suddenly stopped talking. Her eyes were fixed up at the sky and she sat perfectly still. Emma and Cooper were busy looking through the snacks, but Claire noticed the sudden change come over Penny. The red light of the pin was now pulsing, reflecting an eerie glow on Penny's frozen expression.

"Penny," Claire said. "Are you okay?" Penny stayed silent, still looking up at the sky, motionless. "Penny?" Nothing.

Claire looked over toward Mr. Petsky. He was distracted because he was having trouble unfolding his lawn chair. Only a few feet from him, Val was staring directly at Penny. She was grinning. She rolled up the sleeve of her left arm and looked down at it. Claire couldn't see exactly what she was doing. Then she looked back at Penny.

Penny's eyes went wide. She stood up and calmly said, "I'll be right back. I have to go do something." Before Claire could respond, Penny turned and walked off alone into the dark woods.

Claire looked back at Val. Her smile was much bigger.

CHAPTER 6

11:00 P.M.

A single shooting star streaked brightly across the sky.

"Whoa," Cooper said. "Did you guys see that?"

"That's the first of many," Mr. Petsky shouted to the group. He had gotten his chair set up and was relaxing in it, looking up.

Claire couldn't think about the meteor shower right now. It had been a couple of minutes and Penny still hadn't returned from the woods. It made no sense. Penny had just gotten comfortable with them. Why would she just suddenly leave like that?

"I'm worried about Penny," said Claire.

"I'm sure she's fine," said Emma. "She probably just went to go to the bathroom."

"In the woods?" Claire said skeptically.

"Hey, you gotta do what you gotta do," Cooper chimed in, stuffing a cookie into his mouth.

"She's been gone a long time," said Claire. "She might have gotten lost."

"Or she's been abducted by *aliens*," said Cooper, doing his best impression of a movie trailer announcer voice. Claire didn't think his joke was funny. Neither did Emma.

"I think we should go look for her," Claire suggested.

"Mr. Petsky told us not to go into the woods," Cooper replied, reaching his hand into a bag of chips. "I'm sure she'll come back in a minute or two."

"We could tell Mr. Petsky if you're that worried about her," said Emma.

"Yeah," said Claire. "Let's do that. It's freaking me out that she walked away from the group."

The three of them got up and walked over to where their teacher was seated in the lawn chair. Val was right next to him on the grass, pointing up toward the sky and saying something to the teacher that Mr. Petsky seemed to be fascinated by. Other students had gathered around as well to listen to Val.

"That one at the end of the handle on the Big Dipper," said Val, pointing, "is Alkaid. That, over there, is the Virgo constellation, and the brightest star, there, is Spica. And those are Regulus, Delta Leonis, Epsilon Leonis, and Zeta Leonis. They're all part of the Leo constellation."

"I'm impressed, Val," said Mr. Petsky. "You've really done your homework."

Val smiled. "I know all their names because I think it's important to know them." Val paused. "There's one star we can't see," she said.

"Actually," Mr. Petsky replied, "there are millions of stars we can't see. Many are too far away or don't burn brightly enough for their light to reach Earth. The universe is a big place and we can only see a tiny fraction of it, even using telescopes and satellites. In fact, some of the stars we can see aren't really there anymore. They burned out billions of years ago, but their light is only now reaching the Earth."

"I know that," snapped Val. "Those aren't what I'm talking about. There's one that's very close, closer than you think, but we can't see it because it doesn't provide any light."

"You mean a black dwarf?" he said.

"Mr. Petsky?" Claire tried to get the teacher's attention.

"Hold on, Claire." He started addressing the students gathered around. "A black dwarf is what a star becomes after it has burned out and collapsed. Of course, the other way a star can die is by exploding in a supernova." He turned back toward Val. "There aren't any black dwarves anywhere near our solar system, Val. Some scientists don't think black dwarves exist at all. I'm sorry, but I think you're mistaken."

Val smiled. "I'm not talking about a black dwarf," she said. "There's a star very close to us that still burns, but it doesn't create any light. There's life on it—inhabitants that have lived there for thousands of years, long before humans were present on this planet. They collect humans from Earth to power it. It's called the Dark Star."

Mr. Petsky rolled his eyes. "If there were something like that close to our planet, we'd know about it. What you're talking about is just science fiction, Val. There's no such thing as a Dark Star. And there's *definitely* no such thing as aliens."

"Says him," Cooper said under his breath.

"Mr. Petsky," Claire spoke up again. "Penny is—"

"Mr. Petsky," Val interrupted. "You're probably right." She looked at Claire. "While I've got your attention, I brought something that I think might prevent people from getting lost." She opened her bag to show him the dozens of pins inside. "These pins have lights in them that should be just bright enough so we can all see where everyone is but not so bright as to cause light pollution. It's dark here, and I wouldn't want anyone to go missing."

For a second Val's eyes almost looked like they were glowing the same vibrant red as the pins. Claire shook her head in disbelief. *It must just be the reflection*, she thought to herself.

"What a great idea, Val!" said Mr. Petsky. "It was very responsible for you to think of that."

"Mr. Petsky," Claire said. "Penny went into—"

"I already gave a pin to Penny," Val interrupted again.

"But she went—"

"She has a pin," said Val. "She's around."

"Everyone should take one of these pins," Mr. Petsky ordered the students. "It was very smart of you to think about that, Val. Thank you."

Students lined up and, one by one, took a pin out of Val's bag. Emma got in line.

"What are you doing?" said Claire.

"Taking a pin," said Emma. "Why shouldn't I? Mr. Petsky's right. It's a great idea. It's pretty dark up here. What's the big deal? It's just a pin."

"What about Penny?" Claire said. She was getting more upset.

"Val's right. She's got a pin, and I'm sure she'll turn up."

"But she didn't wander off until—"

Emma interrupted her. "She's old enough to go off on her own. You're just being paranoid. It's just a pin. Watch, I'll put one on and nothing will happen."

Claire turned to Cooper. "You're not going to take one, are you?"

"No way," said Cooper. "Val freaks me out. I wouldn't even take *money* from her if she was offering it."

Emma was the last student to take a pin. Once she had hers, Mr. Petsky reached into Val's bag and took one himself. He didn't seem to notice that neither Claire nor Cooper had taken one. All Claire could do was stand by as Emma, the other students, and Mr. Petsky attached the pins to their shirts, the steady red light glowing all around her. She felt queasy watching them do it. There was something unsettling about this whole thing. She still wanted to know where Penny had gone off to. Even though she hadn't known Penny for very long, she seemed just as freaked out as Claire was about being alone up here. There was no way she'd wander away on her own. Claire was convinced it had something to do with the pin Val had given her.

As the students walked back to their chairs and blankets, Claire glanced over at Val. She was still smiling next to Mr. Petsky. That's when Claire noticed that Val wasn't wearing a pin either.

CHAPTER 7

11:15 P.M.

Claire couldn't sit still. She was fidgety and restless. Penny still hadn't come back, and the students were now oddly silent. Some of the red light around Claire started to flicker, the pulsing light dancing across the clearing. The meteor shower was supposed to begin soon, but the extra credit was the last thing on her mind. Something was wrong here. She should never have come. She would have gladly gone to *Alien Wrath* with Cooper rather than be up in these dark hills, surrounded by freaky pins that were handed out by someone she couldn't trust.

"Does it seem quiet to you?" Cooper asked. They were back sitting on Emma's blanket but were no longer touching the snacks. Claire was too nervous to eat, and it seemed that Cooper felt the same way.

"Yeah," Claire agreed. "Everyone stopped talking."

"Not everyone can keep a conversation up like you can, Cooper," Emma said. "At some point most of us run out of things to say."

"Do you still feel okay?" Claire asked, looking at the steady red light at the center of Emma's star pin.

"Yes!" Emma said. "For the last time, I feel fine. It's just a pin, and you're nervous because it's dark up here and all the stories about this place have gone to your head. There's nothing wrong."

"Why isn't Penny back yet?" Claire tried to sound calmer than she felt.

"She probably is back. It's dark. Any of these lights could be her." Emma was getting annoyed, so Claire let the issue go.

She looked around and saw that the students were mostly still and quiet, all looking up toward the sky waiting for the lights to start flying. Mr. Petsky said on the bus that a few meteors would appear before midnight, but the majority would start hitting the atmosphere at twelve o'clock. It should start soon. So far, the only one they'd seen was the one that appeared shortly after Penny walked into the woods.

Two pulsing red lights caught Claire's eye.

In the dark, Claire saw two students from another group rise and begin walking toward the woods. She tapped Cooper on the shoulder and pointed at them. They both watched until the pulsing lights disappeared behind the thick line of trees.

Claire looked back over toward Mr. Petsky. Should she tell him what she just saw? Even through the dark, she could see that Val was still sitting right next to him. She was hunched over looking at her left arm again. Just as Claire was about to say something to Cooper, he said, "Look," and pointed toward the sky. Two more shooting stars streaked through the darkness.

“I’m going to talk to Mr. Petsky,” said Claire. “Something weird is going on.”

“I’ll come with you,” he said. “You coming, Emma?”

“No, I’m not going to contribute to your irrational beliefs,” she said. “I’ll be here when you get back.”

They walked over to their teacher, who was staring up at the sky with a blank look on his face, his red pin slowly glowing brighter and weaker in a steady rhythm.

“Mr. Petsky,” Claire started. “I think two more students went into the woods.”

Mr. Petsky didn’t say anything. He just stared up at the sky and didn’t seem to notice that Claire was even there, much less that she had just spoken to him.

Claire turned to Val. “What are those pins?”

Val rolled her sleeve down before Claire could see what she was doing. They locked eyes with each other. “They’re just pins.”

“Where did you get them?” Claire asked.

Val smiled. "I made them myself," she said. "If you're so concerned with the pins, why don't you wear one? You'll see they aren't anything special, just pins with lights."

"What are you doing on your arm?" Claire couldn't tell if she was getting angry or just panicking.

Val didn't answer. She just stared at Claire, grinning.

"We're not taking your pins," said Cooper. "Why did two more kids just go off into the woods?"

Val was still smiling. "Why don't you ask them?"

"Mr. Petsky," said Claire. "Mr. Petsky!" This time she shook the teacher's shoulder, but he still didn't seem to notice that she was there. He had the same blank stare that Penny had before she wandered away. "What did you do to him?" she asked Val.

Val just continued smiling and looked up at the sky. She didn't say anything.

"Come on," Claire said to Cooper. "We're going to look for those kids in the woods."

11:25 P.M.

For every bit that Claire hated the bluffs, the woods were a thousand times worse. It was much harder to see, and she kept getting poked by sticks and branches. She and Cooper would take a few steps each, then stop and scan the area for the missing students. They made sure to never lose sight of each other or to walk too far past the tree line. They didn't want to lose track of the red lights coming from the rest of the group. If they went too far, they could become lost themselves. Every couple of minutes, they shouted Penny's name but didn't hear any response.

"We're never going to find anyone in here," said Cooper. "I wouldn't be able to find you if you walked ten feet away from me."

"I don't want to give up," said Claire.

"The only thing we're going to do out here is get lost ourselves," he said. "We need to go back. Maybe Emma has an idea."

"Emma doesn't even think anything weird is going on."

"We'll just have to convince her, which seems like it should be getting easier by the minute," said Cooper. "Come on. Let's go back."

Claire took one last look deeper into the woods, desperately hoping Penny's red light would appear and she could stop worrying. She shouted Penny's name one more time and reluctantly agreed to leave the woods.

They made their way out of the forest back toward the clusters of red lights. When they left the tree line, Claire was immediately relieved. Even though they hadn't found Penny, she was grateful to be out of the woods. Cooper was right. The only thing that would have happened in there would have been getting lost themselves. As they walked toward their blanket, Claire's relief about leaving the woods was replaced by concern. It looked like there were fewer red lights than when they'd left.

Something caught her eye—three more lights streaked across the night. The meteor shower was picking up. Soon it would be midnight and bright streaks would fill the sky.

"Uhh, Claire?" Cooper sounded concerned.

"What?"

"Where's Emma?" They had reached the blanket, but Emma was gone.

CHAPTER 8

11:35 P.M.

"Emma! Emma!" Claire and Cooper shouted over and over again. None of the other students seemed to notice their yelling. They were all staring at the sky. All of their pins were pulsing now.

Cooper walked over to the tree line and kept calling for Emma. Claire ran to another group of three students sitting in a circle on a blanket. "Did you see my friend come by here?" The students didn't respond, still looking up. "Her name's Emma. Did you see her?" Still nothing. "Why won't you answer me?" Their pins slowly pulsed red.

The students didn't acknowledge her. She looked up, but the meteor shower hadn't started yet. It was only eleven forty. It wouldn't begin for twenty minutes.

"What are you looking at?"

The three students all turned slowly to face her. All together, they said, "The Dark Star."

"There's no such thing as the Dark Star!" Claire shouted at them. She knew she was panicking now. This was all too much. She wanted to find Emma. She wanted to find Penny. She wanted to go home. She wanted to grab Cooper and run out of the bluffs, down the hills, run away from the dark and into the light of Middleton. She wanted to run away from Val.

"Claire! Claire!" Cooper ran toward her. "I don't think Emma's out there. I've been yelling for her, but she's not answering." He looked at the students. "Did they see her?"

"They won't say," said Claire. "They said they're looking at the Dark Star. They won't say anything else."

"Dark Star?" said Cooper. "The thing Val was talking about?"

"Yeah, do you remember what it was?"

"No, but I remember when Val said it, it sounded familiar. I feel like I've heard of the Dark Star before Val talked about it. I was trying to think of where," said Cooper. "It has to be those pins. That's why everyone is acting so weird. I know I've seen that design before too."

"I think you're right," said Claire. She turned to face the group of three students. "You need to take those pins off," she said to them, but they ignored her. "Take them off!" she shouted again. The students just stared at the sky, blank looks on their faces.

"If they won't do it, I will," said Cooper. He moved toward one of the kids on the blanket and reached at her pin, but the student dodged his hand. Cooper shouted at her to take the pin off her shirt, but she ignored him. He reached again at the pin, but she put her arms up, blocking Cooper's attempt. He tried to take the pin off a student sitting next to her, but he turned away too.

Cooper gave up his struggle. Neither of the students commented on Cooper trying to take their pins. All they did was stare silently at the sky.

"They won't let me take the pins, and I don't want to hurt them," said Cooper.

"It's okay," said Claire. "You tried to help. It's not their fault or yours."

"Yeah," said Cooper. "It's Val's."

Claire turned and saw Val still sitting next to Mr. Petsky. She was looking at the two of them and laughing. She had watched Cooper try and fail to take the pin away from the student. Apparently, she found it funny.

"If she has the answers," said Claire. "Let's go get them from her."

CHAPTER 9

11:39 P.M.

"What are you doing to everyone?" Claire demanded.

Val didn't say anything, didn't even look at Claire. She was calmly seated on the grass next to Mr. Petsky's lawn chair. The teacher was still staring up at the sky like the students.

"Everyone that took one of your pins is acting weird," said Cooper, "and we want to know why."

"They're just pins," Val said, smirking at them. "If there is a problem, it's you. Why would my pins make them act strangely?"

"That's exactly what we want to know," said Claire.

Cooper turned to Mr. Petsky. "What are you looking at?"

The teacher calmly replied, "The Dark Star."

"What is that?" Cooper shouted at Val.

"Leave him alone," said Val. She locked eyes with Claire. "If you're so concerned, why don't you each take a pin? You'll see they're harmless."

"We're not taking your pins!" Cooper shouted.

"Mr. Petsky didn't believe in the Dark Star when you told him about it before. Why would he believe in it now?" Claire was determined to get the answers she wanted out of Val.

Val shrugged and looked away.

Cooper leaned in very close to Val's face. "What is going on? Why is everyone acting so weird?"

Val's smirk turned into an angry grimace. She stood up, forcing Cooper to take a step backward. "They're going to the Dark Star."

"What does that mean?" Cooper had lost any confidence he had the moment Val stood up. She was doing that thing where she stood too close to him, but now it seemed much more aggressive than it had at school, like she might hurt him.

"The Dark Star collects people from this planet," replied Val, taking another step toward Cooper. He tripped on a root and fell backward, staring up into Val's menacing scowl. "It needs them, and your friends have been chosen to be taken away. The Dark Star removes them from your planet."

"You've taken our friends?!" screamed Claire. "How do we bring them back?"

Val turned and sat back down next to Mr. Petsky. "You don't," she said.

CHAPTER 10

11:42 P.M.

Cooper scrambled to his feet and led Claire over near the tree line. Neither of them wanted to be near the glowing lights or Val. Cooper paced back and forth, repeating "Dark Star, Dark Star" over and over again, screwing up his face in concentration.

Claire thought about how Val wasn't wearing a pin. That made her distrust the pins even more.

"What are you doing?" she asked Cooper.

"I'm trying to think," he said. "I know I've heard of the Dark Star before. And the pins . . . I've seen that symbol before too. I'm trying to remember where."

Claire looked up and saw four more shooting stars fly across the dark sky.

"The cult! That's it! The Dark Star cult!" Cooper shouted. "I read about it in a book of myths when I was a kid."

"Who were they?" asked Claire.

"They believed they could travel to another dimension. The book said the cult members all went off on their own one night in connection with—" He paused before looking straight at Claire. "In connection with a meteor shower that was supposed to begin at exactly midnight."

"What happened to them?" Claire asked, afraid to know the answer.

"Their leader showed up a little bit before the cult formed. He told them that he could transport them to another dimension at exactly midnight. When they went away, some people in town got concerned and called the police. Officers went to investigate, but they never found anyone. The whole cult just disappeared."

"At midnight?" Claire said, looking at her phone. "It's 11:44 right now. Do you think everyone's going to vanish at midnight?"

"Maybe," said Cooper. "The police arrived a little bit after midnight, but there was no one there. They searched for the members of the cult for months, but none of them were ever found. They had a symbol too. That's where I'd seen those pins before. The symbol was a black star with a red dot in the middle."

Claire felt a shiver go up her spine. "They just vanished? How is that possible?"

"I don't know," said Cooper. "I remember thinking that it was strange how something so similar could happen here too."

Claire sucked in a quick breath. "What do you mean, it could happen here?"

"Well," Cooper said, still pacing, "I checked the book out after all those students disappeared on that senior camping trip when we were younger. Remember, they went up into the bluffs and—"

"You mean you think the Dark Star cult was in Middleton?!" Claire wracked her brain for anything she could remember from the stories on the news about the disappearances.

"Well, I didn't before. But now . . . now

I don't know what to believe. It can't be real, right? It's just a coincidence. A myth." Cooper didn't sound so sure.

"Wait, so this cult," Claire was trying to piece it all together. "They were going to leave the planet?"

"For what they say was another dimension, yeah."

Claire suddenly realized the connection to the meteor shower. "After Penny disappeared," she said, "we saw a shooting star, right?"

"Yeah," Cooper agreed. "So what?"

"And after those two students with the pulsing pins went into the woods, we saw another two shooting stars."

Claire saw the shock spread across Cooper's face. "You're not saying what I think you're saying, are you?"

"I think the shooting stars are people leaving Earth," she said.

"So that's why Val wanted us to all watch the meteor shower. Nobody will notice a few extra shooting stars on a night like this." Cooper's face had turned pale.

Claire took out her cell phone to call someone—anyone—but there was no signal, just as Mr. Petsky had told them. She held it up as high as she could and saw two more shooting stars—two more people leaving Earth. Still no signal.

"Can you get a signal on your phone?" Claire asked.

Cooper pulled out his phone and looked at the screen. "No," he said. "No service."

"So we're on our own," said Claire. They only had ten minutes before midnight.

CHAPTER 11

11:47 P.M.

"We have to stop Val ourselves," said Claire. "No one's coming to help us."

"How?" Cooper asked. "We barely have any idea what she's doing."

"We know that she's controlling them somehow. She must have some way of giving them orders, telling them to walk off into the woods. If she can make them walk away, maybe she can make them come back."

"What about the ones that have already left Earth?" Cooper paused. "What about Emma?"

Cooper's eyes started to well up, and Claire thought he might cry. "We'll find a way to bring her back," she said.

Just as Claire put her arm around Cooper to comfort him, she saw three more lights flash across the sky—three more students. "Come on," she said. "We don't have much time before midnight, and we're the only ones that can fix this."

Cooper took a deep breath. "Okay," he said.

11:50 P.M.

They walked back to the group to find the rest of the students gathered in a semicircle. In the middle, Val was standing on a rock, shouting to them. "Soon you will all leave this planet and arrive on the Dark Star to be fuel for our world. You will be sacrificed for our survival." Val was looking around the crowd of students, calmly telling them what their fate was. "Do not be afraid. The trip to the Dark Star is cold, but it does not take long." Val smiled at them. "And you have no choice."

The students all responded together: "We will serve the Dark Star." They all said it so calmly, like they'd said it a thousand times before. It made Claire's skin crawl. Claire scanned the group and noticed that only about half of the students were left, and Mr. Petsky was no longer there. The teacher's absence made Claire feel much worse about the situation. Only then did she remember that he had a walkie-talkie that Claire could have used to contact the bus driver. Now that was gone too. "What's the plan?" Cooper asked.

"I don't have one," Claire said. They were crouched behind a rock watching Val shout over the students' heads. "We have to figure out how she's controlling them. That's the only way we'll know how to bring them back."

"Do you think Val is going to come after us?" Cooper sounded scared. She looked over at him and saw that he was sweating a lot.

"I don't think so," she said. "She probably thinks we ran off to get help."

"There's nowhere we could run to get help fast enough."

“I know,” said Claire.

“You’re all very brave!” shouted Val.

“We’re all very brave,” the students said together.

Val raised her arms. “It won’t be long now. At midnight, the rest of you will leave this planet.”

Something caught Claire’s eye. It was Val’s left arm, the one she had the tattoo on. She could see it from here. The tattoo was glowing red. All the squares and lines had lit up. She tapped Cooper on the arm. “Look at her arm,” she said.

Cooper leaned forward and squinted. “It’s glowing red, just like the pins,” he said. “Is that what she’s using to control them?”

“It’s time for two more to go!” Val shouted. She held her left arm in front of her face and tapped a few of the glowing squares. Just then, two more students calmly walked away from the group and into the woods.

“Yeah,” said Claire. “That looks like how she’s doing it.”

“How are we supposed to get to her *arm* without her noticing us?” Cooper asked.

"I don't know," said Claire. "But first thing's first. We need to distract her and get her away from the students, delay her for as long as we can."

"Where do we go, though?"

Claire was wondering that herself. There was really only one place to go. She looked over at the woods, then back at Cooper. He knew what she wanted to do.

"No. You're not thinking what I think you're thinking, are you?"

"There's no other way," she said. "We have to get her away from them. There's no other place to go."

Cooper looked down at the ground and shook his head. "This is a bad idea."

"Do you have a better one?" Cooper shook his head again. "I just don't know how to get her to leave and go in there."

Cooper took another deep breath. "I have an idea."

Before Claire could ask what he was planning to do, Cooper had come out from behind the rock and picked up a small stone.

He was walking toward the group of students and Val.

"Hey, Val!" Cooper shouted. "You're not sending any more of our friends to the Dark Star, not while Claire and I aren't wearing your pins." Cooper wound up and threw the rock at Val. It hit her on the shoulder. She stumbled back and nearly fell in surprise. When she regained her footing, she looked straight at Cooper. Claire didn't think she'd ever seen anyone look so angry. She glared at Cooper for a moment before stepping down from the rock and walking toward them. The closer she got, the faster she started going.

"I think I got her attention," said Cooper. "Is it time to run?"

"Yeah," Claire said. "It's time to run."

CHAPTER 12

11:52 P.M.

Running through the woods was more difficult than Claire had hoped it would be. She was going as fast as she could. Sticks and branches cut her face and arms. Roots and rocks threatened to trip her, but she and Cooper managed to avoid falling.

She made sure to keep an eye on Cooper. If he tripped, she would have to help him—no way would she leave him behind. Val was closing in, and Claire didn't want to think about what would happen if she caught either one of them. If they fell, Val would surely catch up. She didn't think about losing sight of the larger group. They had already run too far to see them anymore. She just wanted to make sure that Val was distracted.

She could barely see five feet in front of her. Claire and Cooper would keep running for as long as they could. The longer they ran, the less time Val had to finish her plan. It was only a few minutes until midnight.

Claire didn't turn to look, but she could hear Val running behind them, crunching and cracking branches. Whatever Val would do if she caught them, it wouldn't be good.

They reached a small clearing, a break in the woods where the trees had thinned out and only a few small bushes had grown. Claire and Cooper both stopped. In front of them was the face of the bluffs, maybe fifty feet tall. The large stone wall loomed up, blocking their path. They couldn't run any farther. They would have to face Val.

As they backed up against the rocks, Val emerged from the woods. She was walking slowly and calmly. She could see that Claire and Cooper were trapped.

"Nowhere to go now," Val said, walking into the clearing. "Can't you see that there's no stopping your friends from going to the Dark Star?" There was something in Val's voice that sounded different. It was deeper, raspier. "I'll give you one more chance." She reached into her pocket and pulled out two pins. "Take these."

"No!" shouted Cooper. "We're not putting those on, and we're not going to let you take our friends!"

"We're going to stop you," Claire added.

Val threw her head back and laughed. There was definitely something wrong with her voice. It sounded more and more like grinding metal. "There's nothing you can do now. At midnight, the rest of your friends will leave this planet to become fuel for mine. How could you possibly stop me?"

"There's two of us," said Cooper. "And only one of you."

Val smirked. "You will wear these pins. If you won't do it yourselves, I'll make you wear them." Val's voice didn't sound human anymore.

Val put her hands in her hair. Slowly, she pulled the skin down her head. It peeled away like tape coming off plastic. She pulled it all the way down to her waist and then stepped out of her skin completely.

With the false human skin in a pile next to her, Val stood before them as she really was: a slimy black creature with bright, glowing red eyes. Her body was covered in uneven scales. She had long, pointed claws for hands and sharp, jagged teeth. She was still smiling.

"You will wear these pins," she repeated. Her voice was now as horrid as her appearance.

Claire looked at the pile of skin that Val had slithered out of. The left arm had flopped out of the pile and the tattoo was still glowing red. Did that mean it was still working? Val's fake skin must have been some sort of remote control that she was using to give orders to the other students.

Claire looked at the glowing tattoo, then at Cooper. He saw it and nodded. He understood.

"You want me to wear a pin?" Claire shouted at the creature. "Come and make me!"

The creature smiled, a glob of clear goo falling from its jaw. "With pleasure."

11:57 P.M.

Claire stepped to the side while Cooper stepped the opposite way. She was backed up against the rock face as Cooper was circling around the clearing to get to the pile of skin.

With nowhere to go and Val nearly within reach, Claire turned and started climbing the rocks. She wouldn't have to get very high up, just high enough so that Val couldn't grab her legs. Even though her whole body was tired from everything that had happened tonight, she climbed as fast as she could.

Claire got high up on the bluff's edge before she turned to look back down. She was out of Val's reach. The creature was below her, looking up. Whatever this thing was, it was still grinning. "You can't run," it said, smiling a little wider. "And I can climb too." It dug its claws into the rock face and started chasing up after Claire.

She looked over at Cooper. He had reached the pile of skin and was holding the tattoo part of it in his hands. It looked like he was randomly pressing the squares that Claire now felt must be buttons Val used to control the students. The creature had claws, so it had the advantage when it came to rock climbing. If Cooper didn't do something soon, Claire was done for.

Claire had climbed too high to just jump back down to the ground, so all she could do was keep climbing up and hope that Val would slip or that a rock would come loose and Val would fall.

Val was much closer. She swiped her claws at Claire and missed by only an inch.

"Hurry up, Coop!" Claire shouted.

"I'm trying! I'm trying!" she heard him shout back.

Claire scrambled further up the wall, now hanging at least thirty feet off the ground. She had just grabbed a good handhold when she felt Val grab her leg. She tried to pull herself up, but Val was pulling her down. This was it. She had failed. Val would send her to the Dark

Star. She was done for. Suddenly, the creature's grip loosened. Val wasn't looking at Claire anymore—she was looking at Cooper. "No!" the monster screamed.

"I think I've got it!" shouted Cooper.

He made one more motion on the tattoo. Val's eyes went blindingly bright. She let out a scream, and a red light appeared on her chest. It grew brighter and brighter. Val let out one final howling wail before the red light in her chest grew so bright that Claire had to turn away. The hand on her leg let go, and when Claire looked back the creature was gone, nowhere to be seen.

"Look!" Cooper shouted. A brilliant red meteor shot across the sky, the brightest one they'd seen all night.

Claire waited for a moment to make sure that Val had really disappeared before she climbed back down the rock face. When she reached the ground, she saw one of the pins. Val had apparently dropped it before climbing up after her. She bent down and picked it up. Its little red light was still pulsing.

She walked over to Cooper who was still messing around with Val's tattoo. "Is she gone?" Claire asked.

"Yeah," said Cooper. "I think so."

Claire checked her phone—one minute to midnight. They'd stopped Val just in time.

"Maybe if I try this," said Cooper as he touched a final glowing square on the tattoo. Claire looked at the pin. It went dark. Just then, Val's false skin turned to goo in Cooper's hands. As it started to slide through his fingers it became more liquid and turned to water on the ground, sinking into the dirt, gone forever.

"Did you deactivate the pins?" Claire asked.

"That's what it looks like," he said with a look of disgust on his face as he began wiping his hands on his pant legs to get the liquid off. Cooper looked up toward the sky. "Look, the meteor shower is starting."

He was right. Stars were flying across the sky, some bright and brilliantly, others dimmer like they were smaller or farther away. Claire relaxed a little. The shower was actually quite beautiful, and with Val gone, Claire could actually enjoy it.

"Is everyone back?"

"There's only one way to find out," Cooper said.

CHAPTER 13

SUNDAY 12:20 A.M.

It took them a while to navigate their way back to the edge of the bluffs. They got turned around once, but eventually they found the edge of the tree line. It was easier to maneuver through the woods when they weren't being chased. Both of them were tired, but they trudged their way back to the group.

They stepped out of the woods to find the bluffs once again packed with their friends and classmates. Everyone was sitting on blankets and lawn chairs, looking up and watching the meteor shower.

"Cooper!" It was Mr. Petsky. "Didn't I tell you specifically not to go in the woods?"

"You're back!" Cooper shouted.

"I'm back?" he replied. "I never left. You're back. I told you not to go in the woods. Now sit down and watch the shower. You too, Claire."

They walked over to where Emma had placed the blanket on the grass. Sure enough, there was Emma sitting on it with a bag of chips. Right next to her, Penny was digging through some cookies.

"There you guys are," Emma said. "Where did you go?"

Claire and Cooper sat down. "We were . . . " Claire hesitated. "We were dealing with Val."

"Who's Val?" Emma asked.

"Val!" Cooper said. "You know, creepy girl, carries a lot of pins, loves science. Oh, she's also a monster, but you weren't there for that."

"What are you talking about?" Emma said. "Is this the plot of one of your movies?"

Claire hugged Emma. "I'm so glad you're back," she said.

"Umm, I didn't go anywhere, but okay, I guess." She smiled at Claire. "Where were you two? One minute you were here, then I turn around and you're both gone."

Claire was just so relieved that Emma had returned that she didn't bother to explain. "We were," she looked at Cooper. "We were seeing if there was a better spot to watch the shower."

"What?" Cooper yelled. "We were fighting a monster! We saved you!"

"Give it a rest, Cooper," Emma said. "That may have worked on me in the second grade, but not now."

"It's really pretty, isn't it?" Penny said. Lights were flashing all across the sky over and over again. Claire wondered if some of them were members of the senior class that disappeared years ago returning home.

"Hello? Claire, would you back me up here? Val was sending you guys to another dimension or planet. She was using those pins. Hey," he looked at Penny and Emma. "What happened to the pins she gave you? Whatever, it doesn't matter. She was sending you guys away one at a time, so Claire and I lured her into—"

"Just drop it, Cooper," Claire interrupted. "No one believes you." She smiled at him and winked. He gave her a confused look, but let it go. He lay down on the blanket and watched the shower.

Claire took a deep breath. She leaned back on the blanket and watched the sky for a while in silence. "You're right, Penny," she said. "It's really pretty."

CHAPTER 14

MONDAY 10:00 A.M.

Claire put books away in her locker and grabbed the ones she needed for science, her next class. For the first time in a long time, she wasn't nervous to go there. She was certain Mr. Petsky would accept her assignment.

Claire spent most of the day before getting what was probably the best sleep of her life. When she woke up, she got straight to work on the extra credit assignment. Not only had she written everything that Mr. Petsky asked for, she'd done a little extra and made a diagram of how a meteor enters and burns up in the atmosphere. She hadn't stopped Val from abducting all those students just to fail science class. This was sure to impress her teacher and solidify a passing grade.

"Claire! Claire!" Cooper was running down the hall. "I've been asking around today, but no one remembers anything. No one remembers Val or the pins or anyone disappearing. It's crazy!"

"Maybe it's best that they don't remember," Claire said. "I kind of wish I didn't."

"I know what you mean," Cooper said. "It's just so weird."

"You love weird."

"I love fake weird, like movies. This is real weird." Some of Claire's books were about to fall out of her locker. Cooper stopped them and shoved them back into their place. "Emma doesn't remember anything either?" Cooper asked.

"I haven't talked to her yet," Claire said.

"Did I hear my name?" It was Emma. "Did you get the extra credit assignment done?" she asked Claire.

Claire pulled it out of a folder and handed it

to Emma. She looked through it for a moment. "Very nice. You'll definitely pass with this." She handed it back.

"What do you remember about going to the bluffs?" Cooper asked Emma as Claire was gathering her stuff and started walking to science class.

"We went up to watch a meteor shower," said Emma. "Claire was freaked out about it, like something would go wrong, but obviously everything turned out fine. Then you got it in your head to start telling monster stories, which was incredibly annoying, but that's the only bad thing that happened."

Cooper looked at Claire. He wanted to tell Emma what really happened, but Claire shook her head.

"Actually, something good happened," Emma continued. "We made a new friend." She turned toward Emma. "Or did you forget about Penny? She's really nice. In fact, I was thinking we should ask her to come see a movie with us this week." She held up a finger in front of Cooper's face. "Not *Alien Wrath*."

"Yeah," Cooper said. "I don't think I want to see that anymore."

They had reached Mr. Petsky's room. "See you guys at lunch?" Claire asked.

"You know it," Cooper said, smiling back at her.

Claire walked in the room. Mr. Petsky was sitting at his desk, looking over some papers. Claire came up to him and handed over her extra credit assignment. "Here you go," she said. "I think you'll be pleasantly surprised."

He looked through it for a moment and said, "Well done. As long as you study hard for the next test, you'll be just fine." He gave her an approving smile, and she grinned back, breathing a sigh of relief. "Take your seats, everyone. Class is about to start."

Claire sat down and opened her book to the chapter she knew they were studying today.

"All right, everyone!" Mr. Petsky stood up in front of the class. "Before we get to today's lesson, we have one order of business that needs to be taken care of. I know it's late in the year, but we have a new student joining us." He gestured to a student that Claire didn't recognize, sitting by the window in the desk that used to be Val's. "This is John. He'll be in this class for the rest of the term."

Claire studied John. She saw something on his left arm—something she recognized.
A tattoo.